ANIMAL CANNIBALS

Ground Squirrels

Sam Hesper

PowerKiDS
press.

New York

Published in 2015 by The Rosen Publishing Group, Inc.
29 East 21st Street, New York, NY 10010

First Edition

Editor: Caitie McAneney
Book Design: Michael J. Flynn

Photo Credits: Cover BMJ/Shutterstock.com; p. 5 smishonja/Shutterstock.com; p. 6 Philip Bird LRPS CPAGB/Shutterstock.com; p. 7 Ian Maton/Shutterstock.com; pp. 8–9 Four Oaks/Shutterstock.com; p. 10 Andrea Izzotti/Shutterstock.com; p. 11 Mint Images/Art Wolfe/Mint Images RF/Getty Images; p. 12 James Simon/Photo Researchers/Getty Images; p. 13 WOLF AVNI/Shutterstock.com; p. 15 Peter Chadwick/Gallo Images/Getty Images; p. 16 Melinda Fawver/Shutterstock.com; p. 17 Wild Art/Shutterstock.com; p. 19 Barrett Hedges/Getty Images; p. 21 Miroslav Hlavko/Shutterstock.com; p. 22 Peter Krejzi/Shutterstock.com.

Library of Congress Cataloging-in-Publication Data

Hesper, Sam, author.
  Ground squirrels / Sam Hesper.
      pages cm. — (Animal cannibals)
  Includes index.
ISBN 978-1-4777-5752-9 (pbk.)
ISBN 978-1-4777-5754-3 (6 pack)
ISBN 978-1-4777-5750-5 (library binding)
1. Ground squirrels—Juvenile literature. I. Title.
QL737.R68H47 2015
599.36'5—dc23
                                    2014028146

Manufactured in the United States of America

CPSIA Compliance Information: Batch #CW15PK: For Further Information contact Rosen Publishing, New York, New York at 1-800-237-9932

Contents

Squirrels Underground

Have you ever seen a squirrel in your backyard? Squirrels are rodents. Rodents are furry **mammals** with four sharp front teeth. They use these teeth for gnawing (NAW-ihng), or chewing on things. Their teeth never stop growing. Squirrels eat bugs, nuts, and seeds.

Ground squirrels have long claws to dig **burrows** underground, where they live most of their life. They do this to stay away from predators. Ground squirrels **protect** themselves by running away and hiding. They will do anything to get food and keep their family safe, even eat other ground squirrels! An animal that eats its own kind is a cannibal.

FOOD FOR THOUGHT

Other rodents are known to be cannibals, too, including mice, rats, and hamsters. This usually happens when there's not enough food around.

This ground squirrel is peeking out of its burrow. It doesn't look like a predator, does it? Don't be fooled!

Ground Squirrel Species

Scientists have found more than 250 **species** of squirrels around the world. They're put into groups, which include ground squirrels, tree squirrels, and flying squirrels. Ground squirrels are **similar** to other kinds of squirrels, but have certain differences. They're also similar to marmots, chipmunks, and prairie dogs.

FOOD FOR THOUGHT

One of the largest ground squirrels is found in the U.S. Southwest. It's the rock ground squirrel, and it can grow to be 12 inches (30 cm) long.

There are 62 species of ground squirrels. Scientists separate ground squirrels into different species depending on their size, color, and other features. The shrew-faced ground squirrel has a long **snout** and tongue to dig for worms and bugs. The Barbary ground squirrel usually has two white stripes on its back and a bushy tail.

A common ground squirrel to find in North America is the 13-lined ground squirrel. It has 13 lines on its back with spots on the dark lines. These features set it apart from other species.

Identifying Ground Squirrels

Certain features **identify** ground squirrels. Adults are about 7 to 12 inches (18 to 30 cm) long, not counting their long tail. Their tail helps them balance. Ground squirrels can be brown, reddish, or grey. Many species have spots or stripes.

Ground squirrels' eyes are high on their head. They have small ears that are often rounded. They also have strong claws for digging. Some ground squirrels have soft, thin fur. Others have thick, rough fur. Differences in fur often depend on how hot or cold the squirrel's surroundings are.

This Cape ground squirrel is using its tail to shade itself from the hot African sun.

Where Are They?

Ground squirrels make their homes in North and South America, Europe, Asia, and Africa. Most ground squirrels live in dry, **temperate** areas, including warm parts of the western United States. Species found in the Southwest include the small white-tailed antelope squirrel and the rock squirrel. You can find them in the dry, rocky Sonoran Desert. The Barbary ground squirrel lives in the deserts of North Africa.

FOOD FOR THOUGHT

Ground squirrels like areas with no grass or very short grass. This way, they can see most predators when they stand on their back legs.

Some ground squirrel species live in tropical areas, which are warm and wet. Several species, such as the red-cheeked squirrel, live in Southeast Asia, mostly in rain forests.

The Arctic ground squirrel lives in the cold Artic. It lives in burrows with hundreds of other ground squirrels to stay warm and safe.

At Home in the Burrow

Many species of ground squirrel spend most of their life underground. If you had a choice between living in a hole or being eaten by a rattlesnake or hawk, you might choose to live underground, too. Sometimes rattlesnakes can slither down into the burrows. Luckily, adult ground squirrels can bite back. Some are even **resistant** to rattlesnake **venom**.

FOOD FOR THOUGHT

Many animals **hibernate** in winter to escape the cold. Some ground squirrels also escape into a summer sleep when it's too hot. This is called estivation.

If you see a hole in the ground, it could be home to a family of ground squirrels!

Ground squirrels do everything in their burrows. They sleep, **mate**, raise babies, and hibernate there. They even have a bathroom! The burrows can be connected to other burrows by tunnels. The opening is often about 4 inches (10 cm) across and is set under logs or rocks to protect the burrow.

Fighting Together

A ground squirrel's predators depend on where it lives. In the desert, predators include hawks, badgers, and snakes. Artic squirrels have to watch out for grizzly bears! When ground squirrels come out of their burrow to look for food, they're careful not to let a predator eat them. Ground squirrels normally come out in groups. Some ground squirrels act as guards. A guard will whistle, chirp, or scream a warning to the others when it sees a predator.

A family of ground squirrels is made up of related females. Family members work together to keep each other safe.

FOOD FOR THOUGHT

A group of squirrels is sometimes called a scurry. Ground squirrels in a scurry keep each other safe!

Ground squirrels warn snakes to stay away from their burrows. They lift their tail and wave it over the snake's head to say, "I'm too big and fast for you to hurt me!"

Ground Squirrel Attack!

Do ground squirrels seem fearsome to you? They might look cute and cuddly, but these animals are predators. Ground squirrels eat nuts, seeds, and fruit, but they also eat flying bugs, worms, grubs, eggs, and even small mice.

The Belding ground squirrel is known to be a cannibal.

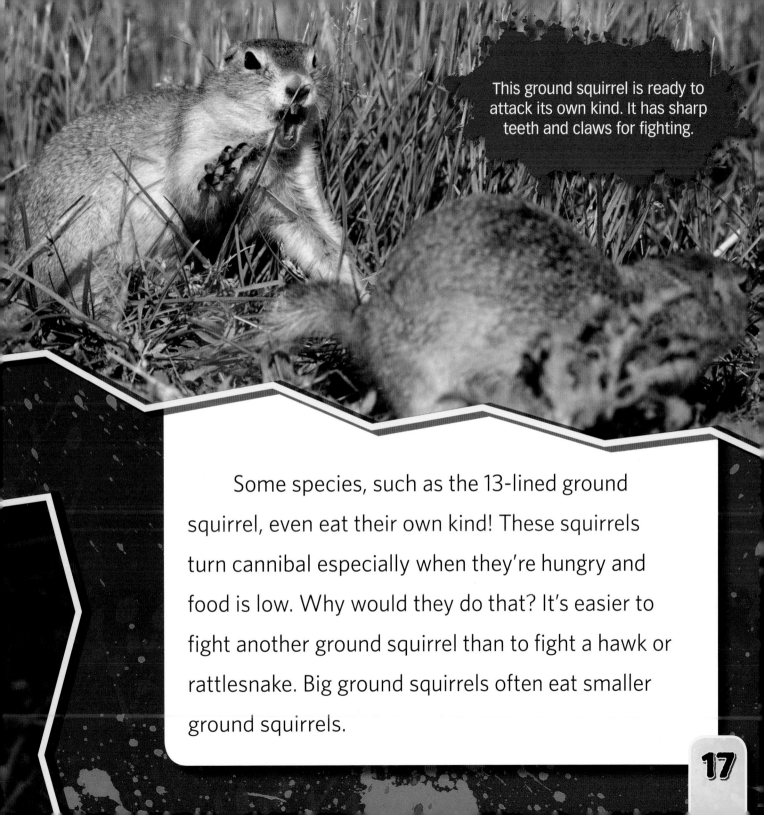

This ground squirrel is ready to attack its own kind. It has sharp teeth and claws for fighting.

Some species, such as the 13-lined ground squirrel, even eat their own kind! These squirrels turn cannibal especially when they're hungry and food is low. Why would they do that? It's easier to fight another ground squirrel than to fight a hawk or rattlesnake. Big ground squirrels often eat smaller ground squirrels.

Mating

Male ground squirrels fight each other for food and to find mates. Since they fight so often, and sometimes kill each other, male ground squirrels usually only live one to two years.

Once a male ground squirrel finds a female, he goes to her burrow to mate. Then, the male leaves the female. In three or four weeks, she gives birth to between two and 13 babies. Baby ground squirrels are blind at birth and have no fur. The mother feeds milk to her babies for about six weeks until they're ready to leave the burrow.

Female ground squirrels usually give birth to one litter, or group of babies, per year. Females live for about three to four years.

Baby Ground Squirrels

After about a month, ground squirrel babies can see and have enough fur to face the outdoors. They leave the burrow to fatten up before hibernating for the winter. They know they have to watch for predators. Babies escape into their burrow as soon as they sense danger.

Ground squirrel babies have to watch out for cannibals of the same species, too. They especially have to avoid adult ground squirrels that aren't in their family. Why would adults hurt other families' babies? They kill others' babies to help their own young survive. They want to make sure their young have enough food.

The world can be a scary place for young ground squirrels. Many predators want them for their next meal!

Ground Squirrels and People

Ground squirrels often live near farms because farmers usually keep the grass or field short. Ground squirrels also like the farm's crops, such as grains and fruit. Farmers raise birds, such as chickens and ducks, to lay eggs. Ground squirrels love to eat all these things!

Farmers think ground squirrels are pests. Ground squirrels carry sicknesses that humans and livestock can catch. Farmers work hard to grow their crops and don't want ground squirrels stealing them. Ground squirrels' burrows can also damage tree roots so trees can't grow. Pests or not, keep an eye out for these cuddly-looking cannibals the next time you see a burrow!

Glossary

burrow: A hole an animal digs in the ground for shelter.

hibernate: To spend the winter in a sleeplike state.

identify: To tell what something is.

mammal: A warm-blooded animal that has a backbone and hair, breathes air, and feeds milk to its young.

mate: To come together to make babies.

protect: To keep safe.

resistant: Not harmed by.

similar: Almost the same as.

snout: An animal's nose and mouth.

species: A group of living things that are all the same kind.

temperate: Not too hot or too cold.

venom: A poison passed by one animal into another through a bite or a sting.

Index

A
adults, 8, 12, 20

B
babies, 13, 18, 19, 20
burrows, 4, 5, 11, 12, 13, 14, 15, 18, 20, 22

C
claws, 4, 8

E
estivation, 12

F
family, 4, 13, 14, 20
females, 14, 18, 19
food, 4, 14, 17, 18, 20
fur, 4, 8, 18, 20

G
guards, 14

H
hibernate, 12, 13, 20

M
males, 18
mammals, 4

P
pests, 22
predators, 4, 5, 10, 14, 16, 20, 21

R
rodents, 4

S
species, 6, 7, 8, 10, 11, 12, 17, 20

T
tail, 7, 8, 9, 10, 15
teeth, 4, 17

Websites

Due to the changing nature of Internet links, PowerKids Press has developed an online list of websites related to the subject of this book. This site is updated regularly. Please use this link to access the list: www.powerkidslinks.com/ancan/grsq